This Book
Belongs To:

# children's Christmas collection

## Table of Contents

# Christmas Park

Written by
Tom Moss

Illustrated by
Ann Iosa

Hi! it's me. My name is Linda but everybody calls me
Button. The town I live in is way up north. There's a park
in our town we call Christmas Park.

Lots of snow falls here—sometimes higher than your head. Most places in town work real hard at pushing the snow out of the way. It's shoveled and plowed and melted. You know, it can be quite a nuisance, but not at Christmas Park.

In Christmas Park it falls on the hill where it makes a slippery slope to sled on. But you don't have to use a sled. Oh no! You can use a saucer. Saucers spin around. You can use an inner tube too, but watch out when they bounce. There are lots of kinds of sleds, but the snow has to be packed down real good for them. Sometimes even a cardboard box will work.

I like to use a toboggan, my personal favorite. A toboggan is big enough to fit all your friends, and it goes very fast. We take it down the middle of the hill and sometimes we slide all the way to the pond.

Yes, that's right, there's a pond in Christmas Park. It freezes over nicely, thank you. It's for skating and sliding and slipping. On the pond you can get together in a long line of skaters and play crack the whip. That's where everyone holds hands and skates faster and faster before turning all of a sudden. The person at the end of the line has to hold on real tight to keep from losing grip when the whip snaps. Usually someone ends up spinning out of control.

I like being on the end.

Another spot in the park is called No Man's Land. In the area between snow fort number one and snow fort number two . . . caution! There are lots of snowballs flying between those two forts. If you walk through there, you could be caught in the middle without a fort. Don't let this happen to you.

For artistic kids, that's me, there is Snowman's Land.
No, not No Man's Land, please don't confuse the two.
Snowman's Land is for making big snow sculptures. No
Man's Land is for getting hit with snowballs.

Anyway, Snowman's Land is a big flat spot in the
western corner of the park where kids and grownups
build everything from little snow lumps with happy faces
to big snow towers that look like a major city.

One time we made tunnels in the snow and pretended we were gophers.

Another time we built a snowman that looked like a big round guy in a bunny suit.

On the north side of the park are the fox and goose trails. This is where lots of kids get together and make a big maze of trails through the snow. One kid is chosen to be the fox and everyone else is a goose. Then the fox has to catch all the geese, and everyone runs away—staying on the trails, of course.

If you get tagged, you have to be a fox too, and help catch the others. This goes on until everyone is a fox except one nervous kid who tries to get to the goose nest without being tagged. To win, the goose has to make it back to the nest, get it?

You can't miss the big Christmas tree with all its colored lights, or the hot chocolate stand. The hot chocolate stand is the perfect place to rest after sledding. It has a beautiful view of the tree. The lights on that tree look as warm as the hot chocolate tastes. But finish your chocolate, it's time to go in. Tomorrow is Christmas!

On Christmas we all go inside to trade presents and stories.

It's time for the park to rest. There are no snow balls
flying or ice skaters skating. Just the snow softly falling
and the tree warmly glowing, as more and more snow
falls on Christmas Park . . . just the way I like it!

# Santa Around the World

Written by
Dave Billman

Illustrated by
Linda Weller

It was a typical December afternoon at Greenville Primary School. Outside the wind sighed softly and the snow gathered in gentle drifts. Inside, Chan and the twins, Kevin and Keesha, were cutting colored paper to make Christmas window decorations. Mina and Sue were drawing Christmas cards. Brian amused himself with a book of cartoons.

Mrs. Anderson entered. "Children, we have a very special visitor today."

"Who is it?" Sue asked eagerly.

"See for yourself!" Mrs. Anderson replied.

In walked a short, fat man with a full, white beard. He was dressed all in red. His cheeks blushed, his eyes twinkled, and his friendly smile brightened the room. They recognized him instantly.

"Santa!" they all exclaimed.

"Hello, children!" Santa replied. "I'm all yours for the next hour. What would you like to talk about?"

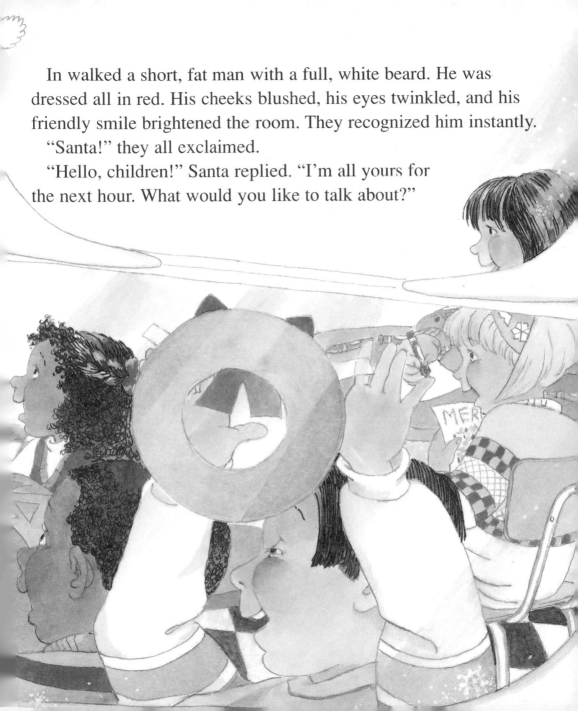

First, the children took turns telling Santa what they wanted for Christmas. Then they followed with the usual questions.

"How do you fit down chimneys?" Chan asked.

Santa replied, "When I exhale I become like a balloon with all the air let out of it. Then I can squeeze into even the tightest places."

"What makes your reindeer fly?" asked Keesha.

"My dear Mrs. Claus makes a wonderful flying potion that my team drinks, and they become as nimble as sparrows."

Brian asked, "Father Christmas, why do you look different in America than you do in England?" Before Santa could answer, Kevin blurted, "He's not 'Father Christmas'— he's Santa Claus!"

"Ho ho ho," laughed Santa. "Brian is right, Kevin. I *am* Father Christmas. I'm also called St. Nicholas and Kriss Kringle." Touching a large globe, Santa told the class, "I have many names and faces around the world."

"To begin, let me tell you about St. Nicholas, who was a holy man a long time ago. He had a very generous heart. He helped the poor—especially children—bringing them food and gifts. He never wanted praise for his kindness, so he disguised himself. Still, the secret got out, and stories of his great deeds spread through Europe.

"Wherever St. Nicholas is still honored, I dress in robes like he wore. Many people believe we are one and the same. Say 'Santa Claus' fast a few times, and you will notice how much it sounds like 'St. Nicholas.' What do you think, children?"

"In Italy, Spain and Holland I arrive by ship and let the reindeer rest. Then I ride a white horse from house to house. Instead of stockings, children leave their shoes out for me to fill with gifts.

"In Czechoslovakia, I simply come down from the sky on a golden rope with a basket of toys for the children.

"In England, I am called Father Christmas. I also look a bit different there, wearing a long, hooded coat of green, black or brown and wearing a crown of holly leaves. Some say I even look rather tall and thin. I travel on foot, but I never run out of presents, just the same."

"I know that," Brian said, "but why do you look so different from place to place?"

"Be patient. I will get to that soon." Santa chuckled.

"Sometimes I have help passing out presents. In Germany, Switzerland, and a few other places I work with Christkindl, who is a messenger for Baby Jesus. She often rides the sleigh in towns while I visit homes deep in the forest. My name, Kriss Kringle, comes from working with her."

Mina added, "My grandpa is German. He says Christkindl is the angel on the Christmas tree!"

"Christkindl is not my only assistant. There is also a fellow called Krampus. Krampus visits only the homes of *bad children*. Instead of toys and candy, he leaves sticks and stones. Sometimes I think he enjoys his work a little too much!

"In Sweden I really show my sense of humor. I am famous for wrapping small gifts in layer upon layer of paper until they appear extremely large!

"In France, I am Père Noël. Danish children see me as a small gnome with a pointed cap, and in Russia they call me 'Grandfather Frost.' To the Chinese I am 'Christmas Old Man.' There is so much more I want to tell you, but I'm running out of time!" Santa exclaimed, spinning the globe gently.

"I'm confused," Sue admitted. Mina, Kevin and Keesha agreed. "You still haven't told us, how can you look different and still be the same?" Brian asked.

"Have you ever noticed how different people see you?" Santa asked. "Maybe your teacher thinks you're smart, but your big brother thinks you're stupid. Your best friend thinks you're funny and yet another classmate thinks you're not. You are still the same person, though, aren't you?"

"I guess I am," Brian said confidently.

"Of course you are! Santa is like that, too. However, because I am magical it is even *more* true for me. I am exactly what people expect me to be. No matter how I look or what customs I follow, I am still the same."

Santa paused, "I really must be going. I have other appointments to keep. I hope you have enjoyed my visit as much as I did." The children agreed that they had.

Then Santa did something curious. He looked out the window and began to wave. When the children turned their heads, there was Santa, now standing outside in his coat and hat.

"Wow," said Sue.

"Awesome!" said Kevin.

Santa smiled, tapped a finger to one side of his nose, and then began to stroll away. As he faded from view, the children could hear the distant sound of sleigh bells.

# The Wonderful Story of Edgar Elf

Written by
Terry Collins

Illustrated by
Sheila Lucas

The date was December 24th and Christmas Eve had arrived at last. As all the boys and girls across the world finished brushing their teeth and putting on their pajamas to prepare for bed,

the elves in Santa's Workshop were busy putting the final touches on toys.

Meanwhile, calm as always, Santa looked at his maps, checking and rechecking the route he would take later that night in his amazing flying sleigh.

Yes, the elves were busy, but none worked harder than Edgar Elf as he readied the sleigh for Santa's big night. Edgar was Santa's Sleigh Master. From the first sleigh he ever crafted, made of the finest oak, to the current sleigh made of shining steel, Edgar had designed and built each one by hand. Past examples of his skill lined the walls of his workshop, each sleigh a reminder of the love and hard work that had gone into creating them.

Like most elves, Edgar was good at making things, but unlike his brothers his talents were not in toy making. Edgar was an engineer. A tinkerer. A mechanic who used his collection of tools and his own elfin abilities to keep Santa's sleigh in top running condition.

Also, since the sleigh was powered by the enchantment of flying reindeer, Edgar was a

master magician. A loose runner could be fixed with a nail and a hammer, but a sick reindeer might need pixie dust and a kind word of encouragement in order to successfully fly across the night sky on Christmas Eve.

Besides swiftness and good handling, Edgar was also concerned with Santa's safety in the sleigh. Some of Edgar's security features included rear turn signals, radar, a driver's side air bag, and even an adjustable seat belt. The seat belt had to be adjustable because Santa's waistline tended to grow at Christmas Eve due to the many glasses of milk and plates of cookies children left out for him to eat.

The clever elf had also used his skills to create two of the most useful gadgets Santa used during his yearly visits: the amazing Chimney Stretcher, which allowed the plump and jolly old Saint Nick easy access into any home; and the Infinite Toy Bag, which let Santa carry toys for every girl and boy in the world in a single sack.

Despite his other inventions, Edgar's number one duty was in the art of sleigh maintenance, for it was with the sleigh he had always done his best work.

owever, after years and years of loyal service as Santa's Sleigh Master, the old elf was ready to retire. Yes, it was time to pass on the sleigh maintenance duties to someone else. Edgar had a young apprentice named Ellen who would soon take over as Sleigh Master.

Ellen was the next generation of elf, skilled in computer design, yet still not afraid to get her hands dirty. Edgar knew Santa's sleigh would be in good hands with Ellen.

So why did he feel so sad?

A blast of cold air swirled across the room as Santa walked into Edgar's workshop.

"Ho-ho-ho! Merry Christmas, Edgar!" Santa boomed.

"Season's greetings, boss," Edgar replied. He always called Santa boss, as a sign of respect.

"Hello, Santa!" Ellen said, and he gave her a wink in response.

"How's my sleigh?" Santa asked the elves. "Ready for the trip?"

"Yes sir!" both elves replied.

am going to miss you, Edgar," Santa said. "You've given me years of hard work. I never had reason to worry knowing you were the one keeping my sleigh in shape. Why, I still remember the stormy night when I nearly collided with a Jumbo Jet! The radar system you installed didn't just save me and the reindeer, Edgar; it saved Christmas for millions of children.

"Why the long face, my friend? After tonight, you get to enjoy yourself, free of responsibilities for my sleigh. Aren't you looking forward to moving to Florida with the other elf retirees?" Santa asked.

"Sure I am, boss," Edgar replied, "but this is my last night on the job and . . . well, I've never actually seen the sleigh in action on Christmas Eve."

And then Santa, who was wise in the ways of little people- elves and children alike- understood.

"Edgar, I have a present for you," Santa said, as he rubbed the side of his cherry-like nose. "Traditionally, I wait until my duties to all of the girls and boys are complete before I give Christmas gifts to my elves, but tonight, you come first."

Edgar, who knew this was indeed a great honor, nodded and then waited.

"Tonight, you shall accompany me in my sleigh," said Santa. "What do you think about that?"

"Edgar . . . ?" Santa said with alarm as he looked down at his longtime Sleigh Master.

"He'll be okay, Santa. I think he's just happy!" Ellen replied.

"Ho-ho! Very good! Best bundle him up, Ellen, for the air can get a mite nippy way up high in my sleigh . . . and I know how Edgar hates the cold. We depart in twenty minutes!"

So Edgar Elf—Santa's Sleigh Master—got his secret wish fulfilled at last . . . the chance to ride in the very sleigh he had designed . . . and to ride on Christmas Eve!

After his big night, Edgar retired to Florida. Sometimes he missed the work of the busy North Pole shop. But usually, he was quite happy relaxing beside a pool, telling the wonderful story of his long career—especially about the Christmas night when he rode through the skies in Santa's sleigh.

The
End

# Christmas
## on Chestnut Street

Written by
Linda Mereness Kleinschmidt

Illustrated by
Karen Loccisano

It was almost Christmas on Chestnut Street. Jennifer sat on her front porch and looked out across the neighborhood. She saw families going to visit Santa, dads bringing home Christmas trees and moms making last minute trips to the mall. Everyone seemed to be in the Christmas spirit. Everyone but Jennifer.

Jennifer crossed her arms and sighed. She knew what was wrong. It had been such a cold December that no one had decorated their houses. The trees on Chestnut Street stood bare and brown. Neighbors' yards lay buried under heaps of snow. There were no twinkling lights, no plastic Santas and no sparkly angels.

Finally Jennifer jumped up and joined her two friends playing in the snow. "Christmas is coming!" she announced. "But does it look like it? No!"

Mandy glanced at Brad. "She has a plan."

"Yeah, she has that look in her eyes again," said Brad.

Jennifer told them her plan. Even Brad liked it. The three of them ran from door to door. Soon, they had all the neighbors talking. By evening, they'd put up a big sign at the end of the block:

LIGHT UP CHESTNUT STREET FOR CHRISTMAS!!
EVERYBODY HELP!

"Everybody but old Finkel," said Brad.
"He'll never participate," said Mandy.
Jennifer hoped they weren't right.

The next few days, almost everybody helped. The first day, Grandpa George climbed up to the top of his evergreen tree on a long ladder. Close to the real stars, he placed a homemade tinsel star with five points of light.

Then Mrs. Appleby, Jennifer's second grade teacher, wanted real people to play Baby Jesus, Mary and Joseph, the Shepherds, and the Three Kings. Mr. Appleby built a manger scene on the corner lot. Mrs. Appleby auditioned everyone—her students, parents and grandparents.

Every day she rehearsed and rehearsed: "Not there! Move to the left please. Can you speak a little louder? I know it's freezing, but we have to do it again!"

Mrs. Harris couldn't go outside because she had a bad cold. So Mr. Harris bought the biggest fresh Christmas wreath anyone had ever seen for her picture window. Then he set up a spotlight that swayed back and forth, scattering slivers of golden light across the snow.

In the evenings, neighbors joined strings of colored lights and hung them across roof eaves and through bare tree branches. Brad's big brother used a pulley to hoist Santa's sleigh and reindeer onto Mr. Weber's rooftop. Finally, the weekend before Christmas, Chestnut Street looked festive.

Jennifer was definitely getting into the Christmas spirit. The only problem was, she hadn't seen Mr. Finkel once. His house was the only one that still looked plain.

On Saturday, Jennifer helped her mom make hot chocolate. Then she, Mandy and Brad took jugs of hot chocolate and plates of cookies up and down Chestnut Street for all the neighbors. Along the way, they saw Mr. Finkelheimer hauling boxes up to his house.

"Mr. Finkelheimer," said Jennifer, "are you going to decorate?"

Mr. Finkelheimer turned and stared at them. Jennifer stepped back. Mandy and Brad stepped back. Mr. Finkelheimer almost never paid attention to kids.

"So you're the one who started this," he said. "Why?"

"It's not Christmas without lights and stuff," said Jennifer.

"Christmas is about lights and plastic Santas?"

Jennifer thought about Mrs. Appleby and her manger scene and Mr. Harris putting up a wreath for Mrs. Harris. "No, it's about everyone working together—so our street is pretty for Christmas."

"Hmphf," said Mr. Finkel. Then he smiled a secret smile and continued dragging his boxes up to the house.

What's he up to? wondered Jennifer.

Monday afternoon, Jennifer forgot all about Mr. Finkel and his plain house as she rushed home from school. She ran down the block, up the porch steps, and into the front family room. Sitting in the bay window was a tall Christmas tree. "It's beautiful," she said.

Along with her mom, Jennifer hung blinking angel lights and
golden ornaments on the tree. Then she placed a blue electric
candle in each window and hung a silver wreath that had been her
mother's long ago on the front door.

"Jenny!" called her dad. Jennifer ran outside.

Her dad was filling paper lunch bags with sand and lining them up along the sidewalk. He handed Jennifer a box of small candles.

"Push a candle down in the sand inside each bag," he directed.

"What are these, Daddy?"

"Luminaria. They're special candles you light from Christmas Eve until Christmas morning. They welcome Christmas."

Finally it was Christmas Eve. Snowflakes floated down silently, gently, resting on roofs and trees and decorations. Jennifer, Mandy and Brad sat on Jennifer's front porch as lamps came on in the windows and the street darkened.

Then it happened . . .

First, Grandpa George's Christmas star burned bright into the night. Then, Mrs. Harris's spotlight lit up her wreath. The Applebys' Nativity scene shone bright, waiting for actors and the sound of carols. Mr. Weber's Santa stood atop his roof, ready to fly. Lights dazzled from almost every house and tree and bush.

On the entire street, only Mr. Finkel's house stood dark.

Suddenly, all the neighbors gasped. Lights shone from the direction of Mr. Finkel's house. Jennifer, Mandy and Brad glanced at each other and took off. They couldn't believe their eyes. Mr. Finkel had decorated! Candy canes and soldiers lined his sidewalk. Strings and strings of lights swung from his house and trees. Toy bears and elves held candles and pounded drums from his yard and rooftop.

Mr. Finkel mingled with the neighbors, smiling at everyone. He even winked at Jennifer.

Jennifer smiled back. So that's why Mr. Finkel had been dragging boxes up to his house, thought Jennifer. He'd been planning to do this all along.

"You had a good plan," said Mandy, when they got back to Jennifer's house. "Christmas wouldn't be Christmas without lights."

"You're right," said Brad. "Now it's Christmas."

"Merry Christmas," Jennifer said, as Mandy and Brad headed home. Then she went inside to get her parents. Together they would light the luminaria to welcome Christmas to Chestnut Street.

# So Many Santas

Written and Illustrated by:
Jennifer King

TO THE ONE
REAL SANTA
I WOULD LIKE

ME
SANTA
NORTH POLE

ME

Santas Santas everywhere. So many Claus I see.
I wonder which of these Santa Claus I'll see
on Christmas Eve?
I see them standing all around,
on streets and inside malls,
sitting, laughing, ringing bells and
waltzing 'round the halls.
There are too many Santas.
Now to which one do I give
this list of all the things I want,
and most important
where I live?

A Santa with a bunch of dogs just went flying by.
Right next to me's a Santa who is
just as short as I.

This Santa on a bicycle is thin as thin can be.
Across the street's a Santa who is caught
up in a tree!

Here comes a Santa, fat and round.
He's had too much to eat!
This Santa's outfit is too big—
you can't even see his feet.
It seems like every way I look-Santas all around.
I guess I'll keep on searching
till the real one is found.

Happy, smiling Santas,
even grouchy Santas too.

That Santa Claus looks kinda sick—
maybe he's got the flu.

There's a Santa Claus with shades on,
in a big Hawaiian shirt.
There's something different 'bout this one—
this Santa's in a SKIRT!

Santas are so colorful,
each different as can be,
but they all still look like
Santa Claus—
so which one of them is HE?
Wait! Here comes a jolly Santa Claus,
full of good old Christmas cheer.
There's something wrong with this one too.
He hasn't got a beard!

A Santa Claus
who's wearing GREEN
is standing over there.

This Santa Claus has ripped his pants—
I see his underwear!

Hey? Do I hear thunder?
What a noise it's made.
OH NO! It's worse than any storm—
SANTAS ON PARADE!!

Santas marching side by side,
red as far as I can see.
But, I haven't seen HIM though,
and he's the only
Claus for me.

I did not find *the* Santa Claus.
But I know I cannot fail
to get this letter to the man.
I think I'll trust the mail.

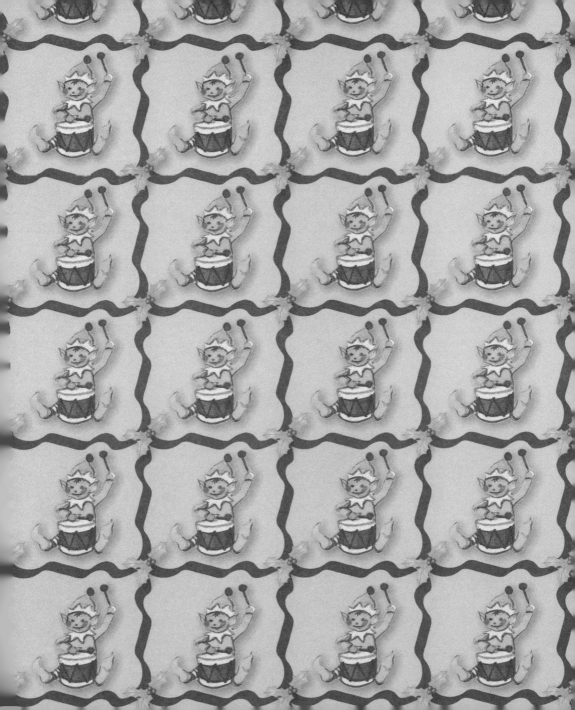

# SANTA'S PET DELIVERY SERVICE

Written by
Laura Rossiter

Illustrated by
Janice Castiglione

It was Christmas Eve, and Santa was on his way around the world, delivering toys and gifts to children everywhere.

Sometimes boys and girls wrote letters asking for pets. And so among the dolls, trains, and trucks, Santa also carried puppies, kittens, bunnies and even guinea pigs!

As Santa floated over the snowy treetops, a tiny black and white puppy nuzzled his ear.

"Ho ho!" he chuckled. "What are you up to, Piper? You'll catch a cold out here!"

Santa knew all of his pets very well, and Piper was always getting into mischief. Santa knew that Piper would have to have a very special home.

Before he knew it, Santa was surrounded by a pile of puppies, some cute little kittens, a bunch of bunnies, and a great many guinea pigs! Piper had opened all of the warm bags and let the animals free. Santa could hardly control the sleigh!

"Mayday! Mayday!" he shouted into his radio. Santa pushed the red alert button, and his sleigh made an emergency landing.

Before long, a tiny red sleigh landed next to Santa's.

"Bradley P. Elf reporting for duty, sir!" shouted the elf, tripping as he stepped out of his sleigh.

"Bradley," said Santa seriously. "We have no time to waste. One of the puppies decided that all of the pets needed a better view. I almost went down!"

"How can I help, sir?" asked the young elf.

"Bradley, I'm late and I can't disappoint the children. I need to put you in charge of delivering the pets this year."

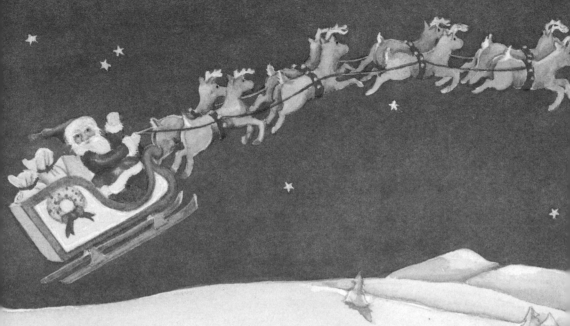

Bradley almost fainted. In charge? Of ALL the pets? What a tough job!

"I'll do my best, sir," Bradley stammered.

"Your best had better be perfect, Bradley. Remember, the children are counting on you."

Santa helped Bradley load the pets into his tiny sleigh and then handed him a long sheet of paper. "It's all here on the list, Bradley. Only the homes where grownups have given permission are allowed to have pets."

Before he could ask any questions, Bradley saw Santa's sleigh floating into the sky.

"Ho-ho-ho!" he heard in the distance. "Merry Christmas!"

Bradley sighed and went to work.

"Hmmm . . ." Bradley murmured, checking the top of the list at his first stop. "This is Amanda's house. She asked for a kitten. Her mother said it was all right. Okay, Mittens, here we go!"

Piper and the other pets watched as Bradley and Mittens disappeared down Amanda's chimney. Before they knew it, he had popped back up and was ready to move on.

"Well, that was easy," said Bradley. "This'll be a snap!"

But it was just the beginning of a long and unusual Christmas Eve for Bradley P. Elf.

In the city, Bradley flew his sleigh between the apartment buildings.

"David wants Gus the guinea pig. But which apartment does David live in? And how do I get in? They don't have a chimney!"

"R-r-r-r! Ruff! Ruff!" barked Piper, his tail wagging excitedly.

"Good idea, Piper!" said Bradley.

Bradley took out a small computer with colorful flashing lights and pushed several buttons. The sleigh automatically lowered to one of the apartment windows.

"This is it," said Bradley. Magically, Bradley popped into the apartment with Gus the guinea pig and back out again before Piper could even wag his tail.

Bradley worked hard all night. It was a long time before he saw the end of Santa's list! "Only a few more pets to go, Piper." Bradley yawned.

Piper whined softly. He wasn't tired at all.

Bradley studied the list. "All of these puppies go to homes in the same block. Let's try the parachutes. What do you think?"

"Ruff!" answered Piper.

Bradley sent ten puppies floating gently through the air, each attached to a parachute shaped like a poinsettia plant! The puppies magically dropped down the right chimneys.

Now it was almost sunrise. Children would be waking soon, and Bradley still had one pet left, a bunny whose name was Blue.

At the last house, Bradley dove headfirst down a chimney, holding Blue. Oops! Someone was coming down the stairs! If Bradley didn't do something quick, she would see him.

Just then, Piper barked down the chimney.

"Is that a puppy?" the girl called to her mother, running back up the stairs.

Bradley gently set Blue in a cage with a bow. Then he magically popped back up the chimney. Sitting on the roof was Piper.

"Good job, Piper!" exclaimed Bradley.

Bradley could hardly keep his eyes open. Santa's list was a blur.
But it looked like there were no more pets to deliver.

The other elves were waiting for him back at the North Pole.
"Congratulations, Bradley!" they shouted, surrounding him.

Bradley was so happy and tired, he thought he was dreaming.

"Bradley," said Santa, "I gave you a big job last night. You
delivered pets all over the world. It was almost a perfect job."

"Almost?" asked Bradley.

"You must have been too tired, Bradley," Santa answered. "You missed the last pet on my list."

Oh no! Who had he missed? Then Bradley saw something moving beneath a blanket in his sleigh. He lifted the blanket—it was Piper! The puppy jumped up and licked Bradley's face. Bradley read the tag on the puppy's collar: "To Bradley, from Santa. P.S. You make a great team!" And from that Christmas on, Bradley and Piper worked together, side by side.

# Christmas is a Time For Giving

A SPECIAL TREAT TO MAKE YOUR CHRISTMAS SWEET!

Written by
Linda Mereness Kleinschmidt

Illustrated by
Linda Graves

It was a few days before Christmas break and the students in Ms. Barnes' class were busy making decorations for their room. Adam, Jeremy and Rifka cut paper snowflakes. Alphonzo, LaShonda and Suzanne colored a big picture of Santa with crayons.

"What can we do for Christmas before school lets out?" asked LaShonda, putting down her crayon. "I want to <u>do</u> something."

"Me too," said Alphonzo. "Cutting snowflakes and stuff is boring."

"It beats math," said Suzanne, whose favorite subject was art and who could color for hours and hours.

Alphonzo looked out the window. "We could make a snowman or a fort or have a massive snowball fight . . ."

"In your dreams," said LaShonda. "Ms. Barnes would never let us play outside."

Jeremy stood up. "Let's plan something together. As class president, I'll be in charge. What should we do?"

LaShonda and Alphonzo rolled their eyes. Jeremy always tried to take over.

"Let's have a Christmas dance," said Rifka, smoothing her hair.

"A dance?!" All the boys looked at her in horror.

"How about going to the rink to play hockey?" said Adam, swinging an imaginary hockey stick.

Now it was the girls' turn to stare at Adam.

"No," said LaShonda. "I think the Christmas spirit means you do something for <u>other</u> people. Not for yourself."

"How about cookies?" said Alphonzo. "My sister made them last year in her class and then they passed them out to people."

Everyone glanced at each other. No one objected.

"Then let's ask Ms. Barnes!" said Jeremy.

The students did just that. In fact, they talked so fast that their teacher could hardly say a word herself.

"Okay, okay," Ms. Barnes laughed. "It sounds like you've all made up your minds. Baking Christmas cookies sounds like a great idea to me, but first we have to figure out a few details."

"Why don't we plan to bake the cookies next Tuesday morning, the last day before break," said Ms. Barnes. "I'll make sure we can use the cafeteria kitchen. But first we have to decide what kind of cookies we should bake and who we should give them to. Then, we have to bring some ingredients from home. So, what kind of cookies do you want?"

The class decided they would bake sugar cookies. Alphonzo would bring in the recipe. "We'll use all of my mom's cookie cutters," he said. "So each one will be different."

"It'll be like an art class using dough," said Suzanne, grinning. "My cookies are going to be angels."

"Mine are going to be flowers," said Rifka.

Adam frowned. "Flowers! Angels! I don't think I'm going to like this."

"Oh, hush," said LaShonda. "Just make yours look like hockey sticks."

Adam and Jeremy volunteered to bring flour, butter, sugar and the other basics for baking. Rifka, Suzanne and LaShonda said they would bring the frosting ingredients and all the dazzles to decorate the cookies.

"And who would be getting these tasty cookies?" said Ms. Barnes.

"Everyone!" the class shouted.

When next Tuesday came around, the class went to the cafeteria kitchen. With the help of Ms. Barnes, everybody measured and mixed and added the ingredients they had brought from home to make Alphonzo's recipe.

On one long table they rolled out the cookie dough, in-between grabbing bits to taste, of course. Then they pressed shaped cookie cutters into the dough and made angels, stars, snowmen, Christmas trees, candy canes, flowers and hockey sticks. Finally they placed the dough on cookie sheets and baked them to a sweet, golden brown, making the whole school smell like a bakery.

As the cookies cooled, everyone made sure they tried plenty of samples. Baking had made them hungry.

"Don't eat all our work," LaShonda reminded everyone. "Or we won't have any cookies to give away."

The students covered each cookie with thick frosting and decorated them with glitter, frosting and sprinkles—white, red, green, stripes, and swirls. Finally, they lined up rows and rows of beautiful Christmas cookies on the cookie sheets.

"Hmmm," hummed Ms. Barnes. "I think we forgot something. Did we ever decide how to wrap all of these cookies?"

The students looked at each other. Then Ms. Barnes surprised them all. She opened up a paper bag filled with plastic sandwich bags, red yarn and Christmas tags.

"What a great idea!" exclaimed Suzanne. "We can write a fancy message on each tag."

"Let's hurry," said Ms. Barnes with a smile. "We have very little time before our holiday."

Shortly before the bell rang that afternoon, the students walked through the halls, carrying baggies that held two cookies each. They gave these presents to their classmates, all the teachers, the principal, the school secretary and the custodian. Of course, they gave the most beautiful one to Ms. Barnes.

"You know," said Adam. "This is almost as much fun as hockey."

"Yeah," said Rifka. "Everyone is so happy to just get a couple of cookies."

"It's because you made them yourselves," said Ms. Barnes. "Everyone likes to get a special present like this—even me! Thank you."

Rifka, Adam and Suzanne took their cookies home on the school bus and gave one to the bus driver. When they got off, they gave cookies to the neighbors on each side of their houses.

And when Jeremy, Alphonzo, and LaShonda walked home, they gave cookies to the crossing guard on the street corner, the shopkeeper at the neighborhood grocery, and the elderly gentleman who lived alone with his dog.

On top of all that, the children saved cookies for their parents, brothers and sisters, aunts, uncles, and grandparents—and maybe one or two for themselves. With each cookie, was a tag that read:

A special treat
To make your Christmas sweet!
Jeremy     Alphonzo
Adam       LaShonda
Suzanne    Rifka

Everyone who received Christmas cookies was surprised and happy. This delighted the students because they now knew that giving was the best Christmas gift of all.

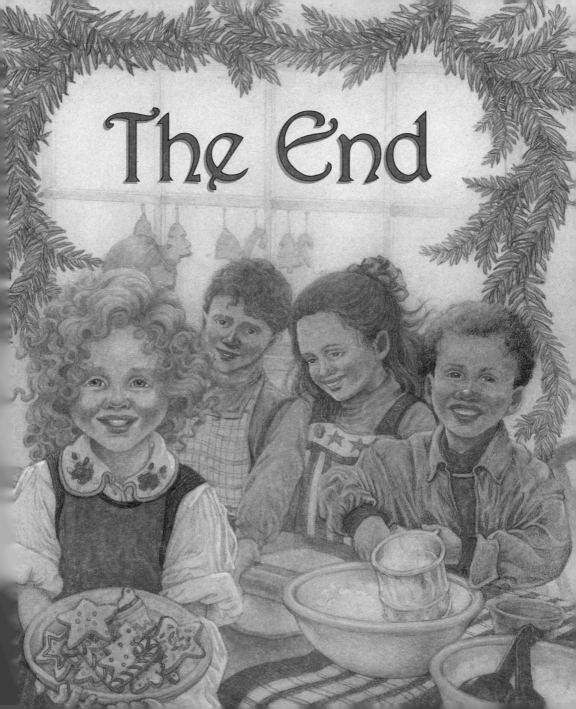

# The End

# The Day Before
# Christmas

Written and Illustrated by
Dave Billman

'Twas the day before Christmas up at the North Pole,
The most hectic of days, with an impossible goal.
The elves put their hats on and readied to go,
While the reindeer excitedly played in the snow.

The roof on the house was covered with white
That glittered like sugar in morning's first light.
Inside was all quiet, the lights were down low.
The kitchen smelled sweet from fresh baking dough.

St. Nick was still sleeping, tucked warmly in bed,
Untroubled by thoughts of the day's work ahead.
Then came a loud ringing he could not ignore—
As he groped for the clock, it crashed to the floor.

Out from the kitchen his wife rapidly came.
"Oh, my goodness! Such an uproar! Who is to blame?
Now I see, my dear husband, it could only be you,
Arising this morning as you usually do."

St. Nick flew from the bed and into his clothes he did hop.
Then he hummed and he laughed all the way to his shop.
The elves hustled and hurried, completing their labors;
Those who were done helped out with their neighbors.

St. Nick carefully inspected all of the toys
To be sure they were ready for good girls and boys.
The wagons had wheels, the dolls all had hair.
There were toys to the ceiling, beyond all compare.

St. Nick marched to the stables and opened the gate.
Now for the reindeer, to check on all eight.
"Get ready for breakfast! It is time that you eat!
Time for the magic that makes you light on your feet!"

St. Nick brought their food and served up the potion
That allows reindeer to fly above hills, fields, and oceans.
The deer ate their fill and went out in the yard
To practice their flying (which *is* kind of hard).

The reindeer all fed, St. Nick was off to his den,
To his big, comfy chair and to pick up his pen.
He had the list of those who were bad or were nice.
He just needed to sit down and check over it twice.

He carefully studied each name on the list,
Until he was sure there were none that he missed.
Concluding this task, to the closet he went
To fetch the toy bag for tonight's big event!

Now, the toy bag was barren, emptied last year,
But it soon would be full of gifts and good cheer.
St. Nick was not worried; he was not concerned.
He lifted the bag, and to the cellar he turned.

He went down the stairs, and he entered a tunnel,
Where the elves dumped the toys down a giant brass funnel.
This funnel was magic and compressed the gifts so
The bag's modest size they would never outgrow.

St. Nick's wife checked the list of what to achieve
Before her good husband would be ready to leave.
The elves polished the sleigh and hitched up the deer.
When they finished these chores, St. Nick did appear.

St. Nick was on schedule, his departure precise.
He kissed his wife once and thanked the elves twice.
When he lifted the presents to their spot in the sleigh,
His staff was so happy they shouted, "Hooray!"

He consulted his maps and checked out his route,
Then climbed to the sleigh and exclaimed with a shout,
"Now, Dasher! Now, Dancer! Now Prancer and Vixen!
On, Comet! On, Cupid! On, Donder and Blitzen!"

The team knew his meaning and dashed off to fly.
Soon they all vanished in the bright, sunset sky.
The day before Christmas was over and done,
What remained was the night flight of incredible fun!

The stars twinkled brightly all over one town
Where streets were quite muffled in winter's white gown.
But at one quiet home the silence was shattered
When St. Nick's swift arrival created a clatter.

The sleigh's noisy landing shook a sleeper within,
Who witnessed what happened, and wrote the tale that begins:
"'Twas the night before Christmas, when all through the house,
Not a creature was stirring, not even a mouse . . ."